J. J Cleveland

The Prophetic Dates

J. J Cleveland

The Prophetic Dates

ISBN/EAN: 9783741183713

Manufactured in Europe, USA, Canada, Australia, Japa

Cover: Foto ©Andreas Hilbeck / pixelio.de

Manufactured and distributed by brebook publishing software
(www.brebook.com)

J. J Cleveland

The Prophetic Dates

PROPHETIC DATES:

OR

THE DAYS, YEARS, T

AND OTHER EPOCHS

SPOKEN OF BY THE PROP

WHICH POINT OUT

The Rise and Fall of Kingdoms a

THE COMING OF CHR

The End of the World, and the Res

By Rev. J. J. Cleveland.

FOR SALE BY REV. J. B. H
1041 Market Street, San Franc
1883.

TABLE OF CONTENTS.

PROPHETIC DATES.

I. INTRODUCTION.

THERE are various prophecies which are evidently designed to represent the duration of certain nations, or the length of the triumphs and the afflictions which shall be the portion of God's people. These periods are given for a purpose. Often they have awakened hope in those who have been weary because of the long delay. It is proper to investigate these epochs. We are deeply interested in them. We desire to know to what they apply, and the time of their beginning and ending.

The knowledge in reference to the fulfillment of prophetic periods ought to be clearer now than when the last prophecy was uttered. In one place Daniel asks, "What shall be the end of these things?" The reply is, "The words are closed up and sealed till the time of the end." By this it is implied that at the time of the end they shall not be closed up and sealed.

Again the instruction to Daniel is, "Shut up the words and seal the book to the time of the end; many shall run to and fro and knowledge shall be increased." By the phrase "knowledge shall be

increased " we think it is declared that at the time of
the end the knowledge of prophecy will be more
complete.

That mighty persecuting nation existing in the
time of John, the last prophet, long since ceased to
exist.   Other strong powers whose dreadful cruelties
the prophets declared, have arisen and flourished,
and have either passed away or fallen into great
feebleness.   Such without his temporal power is the
Pope.   Such is the beast with seven heads and ten
horns, which was ever under the guidance of the
Pope.   Such also are the Mohammedan Arabs and
Turks.   According to the common interpretation of
the prophecy, no other powerful persecuting nation
is threatened.   And it is even contrary to all human
probability that such a power shall arise.

II.   A DAY FOR A YEAR.

In Ezekiel, chapter 4, the prophet was commanded
to lie on his side 430 days, to bear the sins of the
house of Israel, and of Judah.   The Lord says to the
prophet, that he has appointed him each day for a
year.   This is one of the hints we have that leads us
to infer that in prophecy a day is a year.   Every day
that the prophet is to lie on his side represents a
year, in which Israel and Judah shall suffer afflic-
tion.

The application of the prophecy begins, perhaps,
at the time of its utterance about 596 B. C., and
ends 430 years afterward or 166 B. C.   This is the
date of the first triumph of the Asmonean princes.

It was the beginning of liberty which was enjoyed for 120 years or till 46 B. C. At that date Cæsar appoints Antipater governor of Judah. This was the beginning of the Roman dictation, and the end of the Jewish independence.

III. CHASTISEMENT SEVEN TIMES.

In Lev. 26: 27, 28, we have the following: " And if ye will not for all this hearken unto me but walk contrary unto me; then will I walk contrary to you also in fury and I even I will chastise you seven times for your sins."

The term seven means fullness or completion. It is evident that the chosen people have walked contrary unto the Lord, and they have not hearkened unto him. Then, to a great extent, the punishment has come on them. It may be supposed that punishing seven times more for sins, is not always increasing the intensity seven-fold more for the same time, but it is increasing the duration seven times longer.

We suppose that the chastisement lasts seven prophetic or 2520 real years. It consists, in part, in the separation of Israel from their own land, enforced by the power of mighty rulers, and in part, in being kept in subjection to cruel nations while residing at home. In other words it is absence from home, or oppression by alien tyrants at home. This captivity and subjection to alien tyrants in their own land, is often mentioned in the Bible as a great source of the calamities of Israel.

To a great extent this chastisement consists in wandering in the wilderness forty years; in serving their enemies as described in the book of Judges 111 years; after making a deduction of 120 years for the period of freedom under the Asmonean princes, in being brought into subjection to foreign nations from B. C. 606 to A. D. 70; and in· being driven from their land from 70 to 1882. This makes the period of 2520 years. This is twice the 1260 years made notable by being mentioned seven times by the prophets. As the woman or the Christian Church remains in the wilderness 1260 days, or years, so the Jewish Church abides there 2520 days, or years.

If as some think the Anglo-Saxons are descended from the ten tribes, their seven times may begin at their idolatrous defection under Jeroboam, and it ended with the crowning of Edward VI., the first protestant king of England.

In this chapter the Lord declares that he will not utterly cast away his people, but he will remember the covenant of their ancestors.

IV. GOG AND MAGOG OF EZEKIEL.

The highly important prophecy in Ezekiel, chapters 38 and 39, deserves much consideration. It proclaims the exaltation of the sons of Japhet. Till the ascendency of the Medes, about B. C. 636, the sons of Ham and Shem had been supreme. The time is drawing near when the tribes of Japhet are to seize and retain the authority, while those of Ham and Shem are to fall into great feebleness.

"Thus saith the Lord God, art thou he of whom I have spoken in old time by my servants the prophets of Israel which prophesied in those days that I would bring thee against them."

The name Japhet itself is a prophecy, for it means enlargement. Noah's prophecy is in point, "God shall enlarge Japhet, and he shall dwell in the tents of Shem, and Canaan shall be his servants."

Balaam declares, "And ships shall come from the coast of Chittim, and shall afflict Asshur and shall afflict Eber, and he also shall perish forever." Asshur the Assyrians, and Eber the Hebrews, are Shemites. The country represented as Chittim was the abode of the sons of Japhet. It was the southern coast of Europe bordering on the Mediterranean.

Moses speaks of the triumphs of Japhet in this language: "And the Lord shall bring thee into Egypt again with ships." Israel was taken back to Egypt with the ships of the Japhetites.

Again, the Lord speaking through Moses says, concerning Israel, "I will move them to jealousy with those which are not a people, I will provoke them to anger with a foolish nation."

In this prophecy of Ezekiel four of the seven sons of Japhet and two of his grandsons, are directly mentioned as prominent actors. Also by Rosh we think Madai or the Medes is pointed out.

In Lange's Commentary Gog is correctly declared to be an official title. It means chief or king. Gog is chief of the Japhetic nations here mentioned. The Medes introduced the custom of styling their ruler the king of kings. Here a similar title is given to Gog by calling him prince of Rosh. Rosh means chief. It is the same as to say, here is the true king of kings. At the time of the invasion of the Scythians in 636 B. C., though the Medes were the most powerful nation in Asia, they were overcome by these Scythians in a great battle.

The term Rosh, in our translation rendered prince, is by many expositors thought to be a proper name, and it is so rendered by the Septuagint. At the time of the first invasion of the Scythians, the Medes, under Cyaxares, were able to lay siege to Nineveh, the most powerful city in the world. The Medes are fitly styled Rosh, or chief, because that till this invasion of the Scythians they were chief. We think Rosh is the prophetic name for the Medes. They deserve mention on the account of their influence on the world's history. The Medes and Persians were the breast and arms of silver in Nebuchadnezzar's vision.

Gog of the land of Magog, is also termed chief in the same sense in which Nebuchadnezzar in the image as the head of gold is so termed. As in this vision, Nebuchadnezzar is first, so Gog is first in the vision of Ezekiel. The image of the king of Babylon represented all the world ruling nations till the consummation of things. So in Ezekiel's prophecy, the Scythians with the other northern nations, as well as the Medes, the Grecians, and the Romans, are all the Japhetic world ruling nations.

It has been difficult to determine what nations are

designated by Meshech and Tubal. The Chaldee interpreters assert that they are Asia Minor and Italy. This is not improbable.

To meet all the requirements Meshech and Tubal must be allied to each other, as well as to Javan or Greece.

Also, as they are made prominent in prophecy, they should become quite distinguished in history.

It is not improbable that Asia Minor and Italy and perhaps Spain were originally bestowed on Meshech and Tubal, and we know that these countries join the possessions of other of the sons of Japhet, and are in the same latitude with them.

Between Greece and Rome there is a great similarity, in manners, religion, language, and literature.

Asia Minor, at the time that the prophecy was given, was peopled, to a considerable extent, by the Grecians. Several of the cities were enterprising Grecian seaports. Greek colonies were numerous, and of course in these, the language and institutions were those of the mother country. It bore much the same relation to Greece that the United States does to England.

For centuries the Grecian colonies in Asia Minor have been more important than the mother country itself. It was here that the seven churches were addressed by John the last prophet. It was here that Paul labored and to the churches he also directed epistles.

Tubal and Javan are mentioned together by

Isaiah as nations where a remnant of Israel shall be sent, and they are such as had not yet heard of the fame of the Lord. But it is said that Israel shall declare the Lord's glory among them. At first they did not hear the fame of the Lord, but a remnant of Israel was sent, and they declared the glory of the Lord to them.

In the 27th chapter of Ezekiel many nations are spoken of which enrich Tyre by trade. Among these Javan, Tubal and Meshech are mentioned together, and their trade was in persons of men, and in vessels of brass. Such a trade would not be inconsistent with the state of things in Greece, Rome and Asia Minor. They were notable slave-holders. In Greece and her provinces brass was quite abundant. In the vision of Nebuchadnezzar that portion of the image which represents Greece is of brass. The fact of the common use of this metal in Greece is made evident in the writings of Homer.

Meshech and Tubal are mentioned in the 32d chapter of Ezekiel with other nations which have the same fate as Egypt. Egypt is represented as cast down to the nether part of the earth. Pharaoh or Egypt is said to be in the center surrounded by other nations which go down to the pit.

As the ruin of Pharaoh was accomplished among the first, he is laid in the center, and the other successive famous nations, as they fall are laid about him. To go down to the pit means to become base or enfeebled. Pharaoh is comforted because other distinguished hostile nations go down to the same nether parts of the earth.

The first mentioned whose ruin is consummated is Asshur or Assyria. The Assyrians and Babylonians, which were nearly akin to them, were successful oppressors of Egypt.

Elam or Persia is next in order. The Medes and Persians were fierce oppressors of Egypt.

Then Meshech and Tubal are named. This agrees with history, for Greece and Rome were the next oppressors of this ill-fated country, and they took their place in the pit.

Edom comes next in order. The fall of Edom is after that of Greece.

In this scheme, the princes of the north and all the Zidonians are also mentioned. It is reasonable to suppose that the princes of the north are the Mamalukes and the Turks. They afflicted Egypt and their place is the pit. All the Zidonians may stand for the whole of Phœnicia, as it does in J. sh. 12 : 6, and in other portions of the Bible. Tyre is called the daughter of Zidon in Isa. 23 : 12. These maritime towns were not utterly overwhelmed till after the dominion of the crusaders. Then they were destroyed by the Mamalukes of Egypt, that they might not again be useful to the Christians. Mr. Keith says "In the twelfth century Tyre was a great commercial city." This is confirmed by Gibbon. In Smith's dictionary it is declared "This was the turning point in the history of Tyre." After this the prophecy in reference to the utter desolation of Tyre was fulfilled.

In this chapter Meshech and Tubal are said to be the terror of the mighty in the land of the living. This suits the history of Greece and Rome.

Then Gog of the land of Magog is the prince of Rosh or the Medes, because B. C. 636 the Scythians conquered them. Gog of the land of Magog is the prince of Meshech or Asia Minor, because the Cimmerians vanquished it about B. C. 636, and especially because the Turks overcame the Grecian Empire about A. D. 1313.

Also Gog of the land of Magog is called the prince of Tubal or Rome, especially because the Scythian Huns and Alans, in connection with the Goths, Vandals, etc. overcame the Western Roman Empire, thus forming the beast with seven heads and ten horns, which arose out of the sea.

"Sheba and Dedan . . . shall say."

Sheba and Dedan are the Moslem Arabs whose dominion the Turks destroyed. They are represented as remonstrating with the Turks.

"The merchants of Tarshish with all the young lions thereof."

This refers to the Western Roman Empire at the time of the invasion of the Huns, and then of the Scythian Moguls. It also refers to the western nations at the time of the crusades. They expostulate with all these Scythian invaders.

"Persia and Ethiopia and Libya with them.'

These countries were with the Turks and with the most of the Japhetic world-ruling nations.

"Gomer and all his bands, the house of Togarmah of the north quarters, etc."

These were the Goths, Vandals, etc. who were engaged in overthrowing the Western Roman Empire, at the time of the invasion of the Scythian Huns and Alans.

"And I will turn thee back, and leave but the sixth part of thee, and will cause thee to come up from the north parts."

This refers to the Scythian Gog. Coming from the North he attacked the civilized world-ruling nations six different times. The first was B. C. 636. The next was the attack of the Western Roman Empire by the northern hordes about 400. The next was the inroads on the Eastern Empire about 1050, by the Seljukian Turks. Then came the invasion of the Moguls in 1240. The most remarkable of all the attacks was that of the Ottoman Turks in 1313. Lastly about 1400 Tamerlane came unequalled in his cruelty. It was the hand of the Lord that turned back five of these enormous Scythian bands, leaving but the Ottomans or the sixth part. The fanatical zeal of Tamerlane led him exceedingly to desire to cross over into Europe, but he could not obtain ships and was obliged to turn back. The Moguls were intimidated by the vigorous opposition of the Western European nations, and they went back The Seljukian Turks were turned back by the Moguls, and especially by the Crusaders. On the death of Attila his followers without a leader were enfeebled and scattered. And in the great invasion of B. C. 636, on their approach to Egypt, Pharaoh hired them to turn back.

"And thou shalt come from thy place out of the north parts . . . all of them riding upon horses."

The Scythians alone all rode on horses, and they came from the north.

"As a cloud to cover the land."

Gog and Magog mean to cover.

"And I will call for a sword against him throughout all my holy mountains."

Prominent among these swords is that of Stilicho, Actius, Belisarius, Sobieski, and the Crusaders.

"Every man's sword shall be against his brother."

There is an illustration of this strife of brethren in the fierce contests between the Scythians and Cimmerians of B. C. 636, between the Alans and Huns, between the Seljukian Turks, the Mamalukes and Moguls, and between Tamerlane and Bajazet.

"And I will send a fire on Magog and among them that dwell carelessly in the isles."

The isles is Greece, which to a great extent is made up of islands and peninsulas. There the Turks have vanished into smoke. So even in ancient Scythia the inhabitants are greatly enfeebled. (Huc's Travels).

"And they shall spoil those that spoil them, and rob those that robbed them."

This process of spoiling and robbing has been consummated by the sword which the Lord called for against Gog, throughout all his holy mountains. These spoilers we have mentioned above. For many years the Ottoman Turk, in his feebleness has been plundered by the other nations.

" Burn them (the arms) with fire seven years."

According to the usual estimate of prophetic time this is 2520 days, in which a day is taken for a year. This is just twice the notable period 1260 years, or time, times and a half. If this time begins with the first irruption of the Cimmerians and Scythians in B. C. 636, it should end in 1884. Amid the dreadful calamities of the incursions of Gog, the sons of Jacob and Christian Israel have always been able to derive some advantage from them. The burning for seven years of the Armor of the hosts of Gog, by those who dwell in the cities of Israel, is an intimation that for that prophetic period Gog will be a present and warlike oppressor of those cities.

"And seven months shall the house of Israel be burying of them that they may cleanse the land."

This alludes to the period of the various conquering Japhetic nations, from the time of their first conquests of God's people, to the destruction of their authority. But as it is stated in other prophecies, the rule is different with the Romans, the Seljukian Turks and the Ottomans. The prophecy in Daniel 9:26 intimates that the dominion of the Romans was to be lengthened out. With respect to the Turks, it is inferred from Rev. 9:15 that they are to slay men 391 years before their power begins to diminish.

These seven months are 210 years. As usual a month is thirty days, and a day is a year.

Let us see how this agrees with the history of

2

the nations. Whatever connection it may have
with this subject, it is interesting to remark that
the Chaldean-Babylonian monarchy subsisted just
210 years. (See Rollin.)

The dominion of the Medes and Persians began
with the conquest of Babylon B. C. 538, and ended
in B. C. 328, in the complete conquest of the Persian Empire by Alexander the Great. This is 210
years.

The Grecians retained some authority in Palestine
for 210 years, or till John Hyrcanus made an entire
conquest of the whole land.

The conquest of the Western Roman Empire was
made by the Scythians at the period mentioned in
Dan. 9: 26, or A. D. 398. These rude people, the
Goths, Vandals, Saxons, etc., were conquered by
other arms than those of military men. They were
Christianized. Good authorities might be cited
to affirm that in about 210 years or in 606 or 608,
they became assimilated to the Roman Catholic
Christians, in manners, religion, and to a great
extent in language. 606 or 608 is the period of the
rising from the sea. of the beast with seven heads
and ten horns. This is the beast on which the harlot sat, and to which power was given forty-two
months or 1260 years. This power then, should
have ceased in 1866 or at farthest in 1868.

In Rev. 9: 15 four angels are commanded to be
loosed, who in an hour, a day, a month, and a year,
are to slay a third part of men. The prevalent
opinion is that these four destroying angels are the
Turks.

The phrase third part is an allusion to the fact that the Grecian is a third part of the original Roman empire.

The four angels then are four bands of Turks that for an hour, or fifteen days; a day, or one year; a month, or thirty years; and a year, or 360 years; were to act as the triumphant destroyers of the Grecian empire.

The slaying of Tamerlane continued only fourteen days; that of Sarukhan and Aiden for one year, that of the Seljukian Turks for thirty years; while the Ottomans were slayers for 360 years.

In the Eastern empire the career of the slaying of the Seljukian Turks began in 1071; when the emperor Romanus was conquered by the Sultan Alp Arslan. Before the power of this Seljukian evil angel began to diminish, he was to slay men a prophetic month, or thirty years. Then like the other forces of Gog in 210 years his power should be destroyed. In thirty years, or in 1101, the Crusaders and the Grecian emperor Alexius, broke this dominion. Add 210 to 1101 and we have 1311. This is near the era of the rise of the Ottomans and the annihilation of the power of the Seljukians.

There was a separate band which was to slay men for a prophetic day, or a year. In 1312, this band was engaged in vanquishing the Grecian possessions in western Asia Minor. During that year these Turks were dominant, but in process of time they were united with the Ottomans.

In reference to these slayers Gibbon is specific.

He says: "The maritime country from the Propontis to the Mæander and the Isle of Rhodes, so long threatened and so often pillaged, was finally lost about the thirtieth year (1312) of Andronicus the elder. Two Turkish chieftains, Sarukhan and Aiden left their names to their conquests and their conquests to their posterity."

Already Othman with his band of robbers was in the field, and was causing alarm. We place the beginning of his power to slay, in the next year, or in 1313. The Ottoman was the most powerful and successful of all the oppressors. He was to slay men a prophetic year, or 360 years. Add 360 to 1313 and we have the date of the termination of his slaying or triumphs. In 1673 the Poles, under their grand marshal Sobieski, gained a signal victory over the Turks, who never afterwards raised their heads (see Watson's Dictionary, Art. Mohammedanism.) Then the burial of this branch of Gog began in 1673, and should end 210 years afterward, or about 1883.

These repeated instances, of the decadence of Gog, in the stated period of 210 years illustrates the prophecy in Zech. 12 : 3. "And in that day will I make Jerusalem a burdensome stone for all people; all that burden themselves with it shall be cut in pieces, though all the people of the earth be gathered together against it."

The conquest of Bajazet by Tamerlane delayed, for many years, the movement of the Ottomans against Constantinople. But the zeal of Tamerlane led him to attack the fortress of Smyrna which was held by the Christian Rhodian Knights. According to Gibbon he took the place in fourteen days. A prophetic hour is fifteen days. This is the hour mentioned in the prophecy.

Gibbon says: "Smyrna defended by the zeal and courage of the Rhodian Knights, alone deserved the presence of the emperor himself. After an obstinate defence the place was taken by storm. The Moslems of Asia rejoiced in their deliverance from a dangerous and domestic foe; and a parallel was drawn between the two rivals, by observing that Timour in fourteen days had reduced a fortress which had sustained seven years the siege, or at least, the blockade of Bajazet."

V.   GOG AND MAGOG OF REV.

In Rev. 20, mention is again made of Gog and Magog. Nothing is said of Rosh Meshech and Tubal, because at the time of the fulfillment of the prophecy in 1313, heathen Media Macedonia and Rome, had long ceased to be world-ruling powers.

"And I saw an angel come down from heaven, having the key of the bottomless pit, and a great chain in his hand. And he laid hold on the dragon, that old serpent, which is the devil and Satan and bound him a thousand years."

This refers to the downfall of heathen Rome, by the arm of Constantine, in 315. By the Eastern Empire, one thousand literal years were enjoyed of freedom from the oppression of a power like heathen Rome.

"This is the first resurrection."

The first resurrection is freedom for a thousand years from the sway of a cruel and persecuting nation like heathen Rome, and it is the enjoyment during that period, of civil and religious liberty, and of exalted power. The notable Grotius favors a similar explanation.

"On such the second death has no power."

The second death comes not till the thousand years are passed. It is mentioned as an agency, efficient in destroying the beast, the false prophet, and the dragon or Satan.

They are said to be blessed and holy. So the Israelites even, at the time of the destruction of Jerusalem are termed God's holy people. (See Dan. 8: 24).

"Which had not worshiped the beast, neither his image, neither had received his mark upon their foreheads or in their hands."

The Latin Church worshiped the beast, and his image, and received his mark upon their foreheads and in their hands. But the Greek Church was always free from that wickedness.

"But the rest of the dead lived not until the thousand years were finished."

The dead here mentioned are the chosen people in the Western kingdoms who are destitute of civil and religious freedom, and of exalted power. The Eastern Christians, fleeing west from the Turk, carried knowledge and the spirit of freedom with them. The names of Wickliffe in the fourteenth century, and of John Huss and Ziska in the next, are suggestive. But especially, the dead rose to life at the symbolical resurrection, at the great reformation, beginning with Luther.

"And when the thousand years are expired Satan shall be loosed out of his prison, etc."

Satan is loosed in 1313, a thousand years after he was bound, and he is permitted to bring forth against the Grecian Empire his obedient servants the Turks. In this prophecy the thirty years of conquest by the Seljukians seem not to be reckoned.

It is worthy of remark that unexpected agents such as the Crusaders, and the Moguls, for a long time strangely restrained the elsewhere triumphant Turks, from their attack on the Eastern Empire. They must wait till the thousand years are expired.

"Cast into the lake of fire."

The devil here represents the Ottomans whose faithful servants they were. In chapter 12: 9, the devil which represents heathen Rome is said to be cast into the earth; in chapter 20: 3, he is said to be cast into the bottomless pit; but here he is said to be cast into the lake of fire and. brimstone, to be tormented day and night forever and ever. This ends his triumphs.

VI.   THE LITTLE HORN.

The seventh chapter of Daniel contains a concise history of the world monarchies from Nebuchadnezzar till the Ancient of days sits and the saints take the kingdom. A lion with eagles' wings stands for the Babylonians, a bear for the Medes and Persians, a leopard for the Grecians, and a strong and fierce beast without a name for the Romans. With accuracy and success two important powers, the Papal and the Moslem, are described with the same words. This agrees with the practice in other prophecies. There is nothing misleading in this mode, and it suits the design of prophecy, which in general, is not meant to be understood until after its fulfillment.

The ten horns mentioned in this chapter do not belong to the Roman Catholic monster, but to the Roman beast before the division of the empire. As we learn from Rev. 12 : 13, this also had seven heads and ten horns. The Roman Catholic animal was an image of the first.

The old Roman Empire was divided into three parts. This would leave, in round numbers, three of the old horns or kingdoms in each.

Three horns or Western Europe were conquered by the Northern barbarians, who in turn were subjugated by the Papal hierarchy. The completeness of the dominion of the Papists over these nations, is pointed out by the representation of a harlot riding on a beast with seven heads and ten horns.

In another direction, at nearly the same time, three of the ten horns, or kingdoms were plucked up by the roots, by the Moslem Arabs.

Some time after, or about 1313, the three remaining horns were eradicated by the Turks.

This symbol of the Moslem and Papal powers is

said to be a little horn. Again it is said that its look is more stout than its fellows.

The beginning of each was in feebleness, but afterwards great power was attained.

The little horn is said to be diverse from the first. The meaning is that it is unlike the mighty kingdoms before mentioned. With ease this difference may be pointed out.

In this horn were eyes like a man and a mouth speaking words against the Most High. In these respects this horn is diverse from the former mighty powers. In general the beasts which represent these powers are not characterized by the prophets as having eyes and a mouth like a man, but they are spoken of as fierce animals.

Under the fifth trumpet the locusts who stand for the Moslem Arabs, are said to have the face of a man. The Roman hierarchy is styled a man, or a false prophet. Four angels or messengers symbolize the Turks.

The Moslems and the Papists agree with each other, and are diverse from the rest in speaking words, or deliberate blasphemy against the Most High.

The Moslems and the Papists are diverse from the other powers, and are like each other in making religion a pretext for everything.

They are like each other, and diverse from the former great powers in thinking to change times and laws. Changing times and laws means subverting the divine economy.

They have similar success in prevailing against the saints of the Most High.   No other powers succeeded so well.

They are like each other, and diverse from the rest, in growing great out of the corruptions, the one of the Eastern, and the other of the Western Church.

They are like each other, and differ from the rest because their bodies are given to the burning flame. In Rev. it is declared that the place of the Roman Catholic beast, the Moslem dragon, and the Papal false prophet, is in the lake of fire and brimstone. The other great powers do not have this fate.

They agree with each other, and differ from the rest because their dominion continues till the saints take the kingdom.

The same agreement with each other, and diversity from the former great powers, may also be seen in their duration.   Their career begins and ends at nearly the same time, and their period is the noted time, times, and the dividing of time, or 1260 years. The beginn ng of the one is 606, of the other 622. The end of the one was in 1866 or 1868. The end of the other, if the reasoning is correct, should be about 1882.

In the three places in the prophets, where the expression, "time, times and a half" are used, and in the mention of times in our Lord's discourse, in Luke 21: 24, there seems to be a primary reference to the Moslem oppression of 1260 years.

VII. THE 2300 DAYS.

"Then I heard one saint speaking, and another saint said unto that certain saint which spake, how long shall be the vision concerning the daily sacrifice and the transgression of desolation to give both the sanctuary and the host to be trodden under foot? And he said unto me, unto two thousand and three hundred days; then shall the sanctuary be cleansed!" Dan. 8: 13.

By consulting the whole passage we find that the vision begins with the conquest of Babylon by the Medes and Persians B. C. 538, and it ends when the sanctuary and the host cease to be trodden under foot.   But there was a period when the sanctuary and the host were not trodden down. This was the 120 years from the triumph of the Maccabees to the appointment of Antipater as governor.   These Asmonean princes in their spirit and success were like the heroes of the early days of the Jewish commonwealth. They did not allow the sanctuary and the host to be trodden under foot. Since the time of this prophecy, with the exception of these 120 years, Jerusalem has been under the dominion of foreign oppressors.

Deducting 120 from 538 we have 418.   Adding 418 to 1882 we have 2300. If our reasoning is correct, we may conclude that the sanctuary will be cleansed and the sanctuary and the host will cease to be trodden under foot about 1882.

VIII.   THE SEVENTY WEEKS.

In the prophecy in Dan. 9:24–27, which has deservedly received very much attention, the phrases "seventy weeks are determined upon thy people and upon thy holy city," apparently refer to two distinct periods. One of these is seventy weeks or Sabbaths of years, in which every seven Sabbaths is fifty years. According to the reckoning of the Jews, every seven Sabbaths of years introduced the fiftieth year or the holy year of Jubilee. (Lev. 25:8.) A jubilee period is fifty years or seven Sabbaths of years. Then seventy weeks or Sabbaths of years is five hundred years.

The other is seventy weeks of weeks, or seventy jubilee periods, amounting to 3500 years. There are Sabbaths made up not only of seven days, but of seven years, and of jubilee periods. In the original the phrase is not seventy weeks, but seventy sevens.

Daniel had been led to this earnest and long continued inquiry from reading the prophecy of Jeremiah that the Lord would expose Jerusalem to desolation for seventy years. Hence the angel Gabriel takes the term seventy for a text, and he points out the interesting epochs.

The smaller number is the pattern of the larger. Both periods have reference, the one to the first advent of Christ, the other to a time of manifest triumph. The angel is extremely sparing of his words. He never uses two phrases to express the same idea. Determined upon thy holy city refers to one event, and determined upon thy people another.

The smaller period begins with the purification of the temple service in the days of Ezra or B. C. 467. Soon after the walls of the city were built by Nehemiah. Thus it is called a city because it is re-edified, and a holy city because Ezra made pure its daily service. This period terminates with the death and ascension of the Lord in 33.

The phrases "determined upon thy holy city," "to make reconciliation for iniquity," and "to anoint the Most Holy," must manifestly be referred to the shorter period. Christ is the Most Holy, who was anointed, and who made reconciliation for iniquity.

Such passages as "to finish the transgression,"· "to bring in everlasting righteousness," and "to seal up the vision and the prophecy," seem to have only a primary fulfillment in the first period, and their realization is more complete in the second.

The longer term of 3500 years should commence with the going out of Israel from Egypt and the end will be a memorable era in the future.

If for the Exodus we take the common chronology B. C., 1491, the 3500 years will end in 2009. But a passage in the Acts 13 : 20 suggests another system of reckoning. Paul says: "After that he gave unto them judges about the space of 450 years, until Samuel the prophet."

This nearly agrees with Josephus, who in one place makes the time from the Exodus to the building of the temple 592, and in another 612 years.

In Lange's Commentary on this passage we have the following: "We are therefore obliged to assume that Paul has, in this case, received a chronological system which was generally adopted by the learned Jews of his day."

Prof. Strong's Art. Egyptian Chronology, *Methodist Quarterly Review*, July, 1878, says: "If, however, with many of the most recent authorities on biblical chronology, we reject the date (480th year) in 1 Kings 6: 1, and thus allow the book of Judges to be continuous, (as Paul evidently did in Acts 12: 20), instead of making it parallel with itself, we shall have space for the time of the Egyptian Kings as above condensed." (Also see Smith's Dictionary, Art. Chronology.)

If we follow this chronology suggested by the apostle, we shall have 40 years in the wilderness; according to Josephus 25 years for Joshua's administration; eight years for the Elders (Judges 2: 7); and 450 years for the Judges to Samuel included. This makes the period from the Exodus to Saul 523. If this estimate is correct the termination of the 3500 years is not distant.

If we accept this chronology, and for the other dates, take the accepted, the world's great Sabbath is already due. It is a little over 6000 years since the first man. Mindful that a day with the Lord is a thousand years, many in past ages have looked forward to this era with high expectations.

It should not be thought a strange thing that the vision of the prophet should penetrate so far. His visions were all far reaching. They extended till the body of the beast that represented the world-ruling kingdoms is destroyed, and given to the burning flame; till the saints of the Most High take the kingdom; till the stone cut out of the mountain fills the whole earth; and till the Ancient of days sits.

" Know therefore and understand that from the going forth of the commandment to restore and to build Jerusalem unto the Messiah the Prince shall be seven weeks and threescore and two weeks."

Cyrus gave the commandment to restore and to build Jerusalem B. c 538 (See Isa. 44: 28). As every seven weeks is a jubilee period of fifty years seven weeks and threescore and two weeks are nearly 493 years. Sixty-two weeks are nearly 443 years.

In Lange's Commentary, it is said that the terms Messiah the Prince do not refer to Christ, as in the original, if a reference were made to him, the definite article would be employed. Also, in this commentary, it is declared that the Messiah mentioned in the 26th, is not the same as the one mentioned in the 25th verse.

In Isa. 45: 1, Cyrus is called the Lord's Messiah. This is a greater exaltation than to be styled an anointed prince. The Lord's anointed who gave the commandment to restore and to build Jerusalem is Cyrus. The anointed prince (a Messiah) who flourished 493 years afterward, who was the first

Roman who appointed an alien governor over the
Jews, and enforced on them the payment of tribute,
(see Smith's Dictionary), is Julius Cæsar. An
anointed one (a Messiah), who 443 years afterward
was to be cut off and to have nothing is Honorius.

At the end of the designated 493 years, Julius
Cæsar was made perpetual dictator. Plutarch says
of him that he introduced the monarchy. At the
same date also, about B. C. 46, he destroyed the Jewish independence which had been enjoyed 120 years
by appointing as governor the foreigner Antipater.
Josephus enumerates as many as seven decrees
which Cæsar made in reference to the Jews. We
see no impropriety in terming such a person a Messiah (an anointed one), and a Prince.

"And after threescore and two weeks shall Messiah be cut off but not for himself."

Cæsar gave an example, and even a name, to a
long line of succeeding emperors. For so long a
period no nation has ever been ruled by so many
renowned commanders. That period is mentioned
in this prophecy as 62 weeks or 443 years. This
brings us to A. D. 398 or the era of Honorius, the
feeble son of Theodosius, the Great. Of this person
Gibbon says: "The genius of Rome expired with
Theodosius, the last of the successors of Augustus
and Constantine, who appeared in the field at the
head of their armies, and whose authority was uni-
versally acknowledged throughout the whole extent
of the empire."

On the death of Theodosius, Honorius sat on the

throne of the Western Empire. Unlike the first Cæsar he is not called a Prince, but simply an anointed one. This is said of him that he shall be cut off. The phrase "but not for himself" in the margin is rendered "and shall have nothing."

This is the time when the sixth head of the beast with seven heads and ten horns, was wounded to death, whose deadly wound was healed. It was healed in 606 by the establishment of the Roman Catholic dominion.

"And the people of the prince that shall come shall destroy the city and the sanctuary."

The prince is the Roman Emperor and the people are the Romans. The reference is to the destruction of Jerusalem which was consummated A. D. 70.

"And he shall confirm the covenant with many for one week." This is a week of seven years. The person who confirms the covenant is the Roman Emperor. The time probably is the first destruction of the city under Titus, and the second under Adrian.

"And in the midst of the week he shall cause the sacrifice and oblation to cease."

The sacrifice and oblation ceased with the destruction of the city and the temple in 70. It was in the midst of the week or after more than three years of war.

"For the overspreading of abominations . . . poured upon the desolate."

The overspreading of abominations has continued to the present. They will be continued till that

3

determined shall be poured upon the desolate or the desolator, as it is rendered in the margin. The present and probably the last desolator is the Turk. We have reason to hope that when the dominion of the Turk shall be done away, the overspreading of abominations shall also cease.

XI. TIME OF THE END.

"And at the time of the end shall the king of the south push at him; and the king of the north shall come against him like a whirlwind, etc." (Dan. 11: 30).

With good reason many conclude that the king of the south is the Moslem Arabs, and the king of the north is the Turks. The king or kingdom which they are said to push at, and to come against, is the Roman. The connection intimates this, for the Roman power had just been mentioned, at first as heathen Rome, which took away the Hebrews' daily sacrifice, and set up the abomination that maketh desolate; and then as Papal Rome, of whom it is said that " He shall do according to his will; and he shall exalt himself, and magnify himself above every god and shall speak marvelous things against the God of gods."

The Arabs and Turks succeeded in vanquishing two-thirds of the old Roman empire, and they often attacked the remaining third.

In reference to these wonderful prophecies in this chapter, two questions are asked, the first by an angel, the second by Daniel himself. The one asks,

"How long to the end of these wonders?" The other asks, "What the end of these?" They would not ask about the same thing. The fact that the answers are diverse shows that the questions relate to different events.

The first answer is, "It shall be for a time, times, and a half; and when he shall have accomplished to scatter the power of the holy people all these things shall be finished."

This probably relates to the dominion of the Moslem Arabs and Turks. Where they hold authority, the power of the holy people is scattered. A time is 360 days, or a year; times is 720 days, or two years; half a time is 180 days or half a year. The whole period is equal to 1260 days or years.

The era from which the Moslems reckon time is 622. If this is the beginning, the end will be in 1882. This coincides with other prophecies which refer to the end of the Moslem rule.

The second question appears to have a reference to the duration of the persecutions of heathen and Papal Rome. In this prophecy these persecutions are distinctly mentioned. Of God's people it is said, "They shall fall by the sword, and by flame, by captivity and by spoil many days." This would awaken in Daniel deep interest and inquiry.

The fact that the time begins with the forcible termination of the religious service of the Hebrews at the destruction of Jerusalem, leads us to conclud that the answer points out the period of the Roman tyranny.

"And from the time that the daily sacrifice shall be taken away and the abomination that maketh desolate set up, there shall be a thousand two hundred and ninety days."

Jerusalem was encompassed with armies in 67. This is equivalent to setting up the abomination that maketh desolate. But there was an era of freedom from the favor of Constantine 313, to the temporal power of the Pope 606, or 293 years. This must be deducted. Then the termination of the 1290 years is in 1650. This brings us to Cromwell whose rule was more excellent than had been known hitherto in Europe. In 1648, the thirty years' war was concluded, and the treaty of Westphalia was consummated. By this treaty freedom of conscience is granted to all. This is the beginning of the end of persecution. Lyman says that "It is the basis of all other treaties."

"Blessed is he that waiteth to the thousand three hundred and five and thirty days."

This adds forty-five years and brings us to 1695.

The treaty of Ryswick was concluded in 1697. This was another occasion of triumph to the godly. Macaulay remarks that since the restoration there had not been such a manifestation of joy in England. James II. of England had violated every compact, and had undertaken to do away with civil and religious liberty, but by this treaty his hopes are blasted. In 1685, Louis XIV. of France, displayed the ancient spirit of persecution by revoking the edict of Nantes by which more than half a million of the best citizens were forced into foreign lands. But from this era even in France such cruelties must cease. At this time Peter the Great is on the throne of Russia, and the progress of this great nation fairly begins. The republican king, William III., rules in England, and no one better than he knew how to teach princes to reign. The Turks have begun to lose their power, and they forever cease to be the terror of the Christian nations. It may be truly said, Blessed is he that waiteth and cometh to 1695. From this era throughout christendom all fearful persecution ceases. As shown in 2 Thess., 4:17, God's people are henceforth to enjoy supreme power.

By some expositors it is thought that the taking away the daily sacrifice, refers to some noted tyrannical act by which the church is oppressed. They claim that the injurious decrees of Justinian in 533, and of Phocas in 606, are such acts. Indeed it may be proper to reckon from 533 as a shadow of the prophecy whose fulfillment truly begins in 67.

If we add 533 to 1290 we have 1823. This is the termination of the long-continued and fierce conflict for the enjoyment of freedom. This began in the United States in 1775, where it terminated successfully. It broke out in 1789 in France, and to a great extent repressed the tyranny of the rulers in Europe. The contagion, with all its violence, spread to the Spanish-American States, and in 1823 resulted in the enjoyment of republican institutions. 1823 is also the renowned era of freedom to the Greeks.

If we add 533 to the last period or to 1335 we
have 1868. This date will forever be memorable as
the termination of the power of the beast with seven
heads and ten horns, on which was seated the
harlot.   In other words, it is the end of the temporal power of the Pope.

"Thou shalt stand in thy lot at the end of the
days."

The end of the days is at the time of the political
supremacy of the Protestant nations, which are the
true Israel.   Then Daniel shall stand in his lot as
before Christ's ministry, Elijah stood in his lot, in
the person of John the Baptist.

X.   THE TWO WITNESSES.

"But the court which is without, leave out and
measure it not." Rev. 11:7.

The court which is not measured may refer to
every portion of the Roman Catholic dominion
where deluding religious services are enforced. The
forty-two months during which the Gentiles tread
under foot the holy city is 1260 days, or years.
The holy city is the former righteous dominion
which was usurped by the corrupt Roman Catholic
power. The forty-two months begin about 606,
and end about 1866. Soon after 1866, owing to the
destruction of the beast, the pure word of God has
been preached in Roman Catholic countries, and
even in Rome itself, and none can hinder it.

The fact that the Gentiles abide in the court
though they tread under foot the holy city, shows

that they have some knowledge of true religion. This answers to the condition of the Latin Church.

The two witnesses are the Christian ministers who amid fierce persecution preached the word. The Lord sent out his apostles by twos. The time of their persecution is 1260 years.

They have the power of Moses and Elijah to turn waters into blood, and to cause fire to consume their enemies. When they have finished their testimony the Roman Beast makes war against and kills them. Their dead bodies lie in the street of the great city which spiritually is called Sodom and Egypt, where our Lord was crucified. Those who dwell on the earth rejoice at their death.

The witnesses began their testimony at the time of Stephen's persecution about 34. They were slain at the Lateran council, May 5, 1514. The orator of that council declared: "There is an end of resistance to the papal rule and religion." They rose again in three days and a half, or three years and a half, in Oct. 31, 1517, when Luther posted his theses at Wittenberg. The tenth part of the city falling was one of the horns of the beast or England, which was separated from the Latin Church. The great earthquake was the reformation.

From this period there must be deducted 220 years, or from 313 to 533. During this 220 years the witnesses were not clothed in sackcloth.

It may be remarked that owing to the prominence of these witnesses, they were more easily subjected to the power of tyrants than was the church whose history is given in the twelfth chapter. Hence their disabilities began in 34 instead of 67, and again in 533 instead of 606.

Also a friendly power could protect these witnesses with more facility than it could the whole church. Hence 1517 was the period of freedom for the witnesses, but the church was oppressed till 1620.

XI. THE WOMAN IN THE WILDERNESS.

"And there appeared a great wonder in heaven; a woman clothed with the sun, and the moon under her feet," etc. Rev. 12: 1.

This woman is the church as she existed at the birth of Christ. Sun is the highest world power, which at this time was the great red dragon with seven heads and ten horns, or heathen Rome.

That the woman is clothed with the sun implies that the chief government interfered in her affairs. Herod, the Roman ruler, built the temple; greatly promoted internal improvement, and in many modes strove to please the Jews.

The moon under her feet implies that this church was enjoying the spiritual authority.

The crown of twelve stars is a reference to the twelve tribes of Israel.

The woman brought forth a man child, who was to rule all nations with a rod of iron. This child is Christ.

The dragon sought to destroy the child as soon as it was born.

Herod sought to destroy the child, and the Roman governor, Pilate, caused the Lord to be crucified.

Her child was caught up to God and his throne.

This is a literal description of the ascension of Christ to heaven.

The woman is represented as fleeing into the wilderness. It is the Christian Church which thus flees. The time of the flight is 67. The Lord instructs his disciples that when they shall see Jerusalem encompassed with armies, they must hasten and flee to the mountains. This took place in 67. The termination of the time of the abode in the wilderness is 1620. This is the date of the landing of the pilgrims at Plymouth. Here, for the first time in many centuries, the church found rest, and by the blessing of God she has enjoyed it here ever since. "A little one becomes a thousand and a small one a strong nation."

In this period from 67 to 1620 we deduct the memorable years from 313 to 606, or from the favorable decree of Constantine, to the disastrous one of Phocas. During these 293 years the church was not separated and hunted down.

The war in heaven refers to the contest between Christianity and paganism. The act of casting the dragon into the earth refers to the overthrow of heathenism and the establishment of Christianity in its place. This was begun by Constantine.

"And when the dragon saw that he was cast into the earth," etc. The dragon when he was cast into the earth is the guide of the Moslem Arabs and

Turks.   These were as cruel in war, as debased by their social vices, and as besotted by ignorance and superstition, as were the pagan Romans.   Their rulers were more oppressive.   They deserve to be characterized as the dragon and Satan.

"And to the woman were given two wings of a great eagle."

This branch of the church is obliged to hasten and avoid the persecutions of the Moslems.   She is nourished for a time and times, and half a time, from the face of the serpent.   This is 1260 years.

The Mohammedan era began in 622.   Then the termination of the flight of the woman from the face of the Moslem serpent will be in 1882.   In this empire given over to Satan, the church does not yet enjoy freedom.

"And the serpent cast out of his mouth water as a flood after the woman," etc.   The flood symbolizes invading forces.

"And the earth opened her mouth and swallowed up the flood," etc.   This was especially illustrated by the attack of Charles Martel on the invading forces of the Arabs, and of Solieski on the forces of the Turks.

XII.   THE BEAST WITH TEN HORNS.

"And I stood upon the sand of the sea and saw a beast rise up out of the sea, having seven heads and ten horns, and upon his horns ten crowns, and upon his heads the name of blasphemy."   Rev. 13: 1.

This beast is like the four seen by Daniel and it

is their successor. Like them it came out of the sea.
The first beast of Daniel was like a lion. This has
a lion's mouth. The second was like a bear. This
has feet like a bear. The third was like a leopard.
This also is like a leopard.

The dragon gives this beast his power and his
seat and great authority. The dragon is pagan
Rome.

One of the heads of this beast was as it were
wounded to death, but the deadly wound was
healed. It was wounded to death in the reign of
the feeble Honorius. The deadly wound was
healed by the rising from the sea of this beast which
we are now describing. This was about 606.

"And power was given unto him to continue
forty-two months." The word translated to continue means to do or to execute. Forty-two months
is twelve hundred and sixty days or years. The
fulfillment of this prophecy gives us a chance, with
more accuracy, to estimate when this time begins.
The Pope lost his temporal power in 1868. Since
then this beast has been powerless. This makes
his beginning as acting in association with the
sacerdotal power near the notable era 606.

In view of the fact that the bull of the Pope for
the convocation of an Ecumenical Council issued in
1868 does not invite sovereigns to sit in that council,
Elliott states, that it is " An admission of the completed ending of the period of the kings of Western
Christendom spiritually subjecting the power of
their kingdoms to him; that is of the completed
ending of twelve hundred and sixty years."

XIII.   THE BEAST WITH TWO HORNS.

The beast with two horns described in Rev. 12:
11, is the Dominicans and Franciscans.   And, in
process of time, the Jesuits, also a monastic order,
took his place.   It is the same beast.   The Jesuits
were an afterthought, suited to the changed times
and like the Dominicans and Franciscans the special
object was to infuse new life into the Roman Catholic beast.

In the beginning of the thirteenth century, the
pure word, preached, especially by the Albigenses,
was becoming quite efficient and the old ten-horned
Roman Catholic beast was slow and awkward in
suppressing it.   So this new animal was demanded.
It is said that he exercised all the power of the first
beast before him.   These monkish fraternities did
exercise this authority.

Also after the reformation, the old beast was so
laggard and unsuccessful in dealing with the reformers, that it was thought needful to enthrone the
Jesuits.

This beast is said to come out of the earth.   This
implies that he came out of the Roman Catholic
world.

The horns are those of a lamb, but he spoke as a
dragon.   The idea is that he counterfeited the
appearance of a lamb, while he had the disposition
of the old Pagan Roman dragon.   Though the
priests of these orders instituted the cruelties here

mentioned, they hypocritically shifted the responsibility on the secular authority.

The image of the Roman Catholic beast was the inquisition. This had the power both to speak, and to cause that all who did not worship it should be killed. By this it is implied that all organized bodies as well as individuals, that did not pay the highest deference to the inquisition were obliged to succumb to it. It is the death of organized bodies as well as of individuals that is here mentioned.

The causing fire to come down from heaven is an allusion to the fire that Elijah caused to fall on his enemies to destroy them. Heaven here represents tha· exalted place, from which descends the highest human authority. This is the fire of man's wrath and it consumes the good. The multitude of the martyrs since the year 1200 attests the ravage of this flame. In three hundred years more than 1,500,000 endured the death of martyrs.

The causing that all who have not the mark of the beast shall neither buy nor sell is a reference to the exclusion, in all places where the beast has power, of the so-called heretics, from civil and religious privileges.

The miracles by which he deceived those who dwell on the earth, or the Roman Catholic world, were not so much attempted imitations of the miracles of Christ, as the making an image of the beast, and giving life to it, and causing fire to fall from heaven.

Following a common and appropriate explanation we find the number 666 in the Greek word λατεινος

meaning Latin. According to the method of the
Grecians, taking each letter for a number, we have
666. It is a Latin beast. The powerful monastic
fraternities have only attained their greatest success
in the Latin-speaking countries. The language is re-
garded so important that always it has been used in
the worship, forming most of the service, and it has
been a choice agency to keep in darkness the multitude who do not understand a word of it.

The number also has a reference to the duration
of this power which is 666 years. Lyman makes
the inquisition begin at 1204. Perhaps the beast
began his existence at the same time. Then the
end should have been in 1870 or near the time of
the fall of the ten-horned animal. For obvious rea-
sons they should both go down together.

The false prophet still lives, but he differs from
this two-horned animal, in that he has now no power
to make an image of the ten-horned beast, or to give
life to it, or to cause fire to fall from heaven. So in
this book, the false prophet is spoken of as efficient
in the crusades. But he had not yet assumed the
body and horns of a beast.

As it is in point we will quote from Mosheim's
History: "During three centuries these two fraternities (the Dominican and Franciscan) governed,
with an almost universal and absolute sway, both
State and Church, filled the highest posts both ecclesiastical and civil, taught in the universities and
churches with an authority before which all opposition was silent, and maintained the pretended

majesty and prerogatives of the Roman pontiffs, against kings, princes, bishops, and heretics, with incredible ardor and equal success. The Dominicans and Franciscans were, before the Reformation, what the Jesuits became after that happy and glorious event, the very soul of the hierarchy, the engines of State, the secret springs of all the motions of both, and the authors or directors of every great and important event both in the religious and political world." And again: "These two orders restored the church from that declining condition in which it had been languishing for many years, by the zeal and activity with which they set themselves to discover and extirpate heretics, to undertake various negotiations and embassies for the interest of the hierarchy, and to confirm the wavering multitude in an implicit obedience to the Roman pontiffs."

XIV. THE SEALS.

In Rev. VI. the first six seals are designed to represent the most striking characteristics of the different leading tyrannical governments, or the different phases of the same government, during the whole period covered by this prophecy.

The first seal, introducing a rider on a white horse, represents the long line of renowned and conquering emperors, from Julius Cæsar, B. C. 46, till early in the reign of Honorius or 398. This is the threescore and two weeks mentioned in Dan. 9: 26. It is fitly said "He went forth conquering and to conquer."

The second seal represents the dominion of the Goths, Vandals, Saxons, etc., in the Western Empire from 398 till about 606, or till they were Christianized. Power was given to this rider to take peace from the earth, and that they should kill one another, and there was given unto him a great sword. Contentions were common between the different tribes, and by their successful attack on the Western Roman Empire they took peace from the earth. This is the power that smote to death the sixth head of the beast whose deadly wound was healed about 606, by the rise of the ten-horned beast and the papacy.

The rider shown by opening the third seal, sits on a black horse, and in his hand there is a pair of balances. A voice is heard saying: "A measure of wheat for a penny, and three measures of barley for a penny, and see thou hurt not the oil and the wine."

The ruler described here does not promote thrift, and he swallows the goods of the people by exactions.

The oppression is made apparent when we consider that a measure of wheat is essential for one's daily food, and the penny that purchased it was all that could be obtained for a day's labor.

There is also an allusion to spiritual tyranny. The bread of life and the wine of the kingdom are enjoyed only amid humiliating disabilities.

This rider represents the peculiarities of the Asiatic rulers, which at first afflicted a part of the Eastern Christian Empire, and at length the whole of it. The oppression began with the Persian Chosroes III., who about the year 600 overran a considerable portion of the eastern Christian dominion. It has continued under the Moslem Arabs and Turks even to the present day. Oil and wine abound where these tyrants rule.

When the fourth seal was opened a pale horse is seen. The name of the rider is death, and hell followed with him. He is called death, not because he destroys natural life, but the power and life of godliness, and freedom and true science.

Hell, or the grave, follows. In the grave is buried out of sight every civil or religious institution which promotes human freedom or godliness. Righteous men also are ingulfed by it. The power of hell or the grave was manifestly displayed under the next seal, which indeed is the same government but under a later and sterner rule. The inquisition was the very personification of the grave.

In this prophecy it is said that death and hell were cast into the lake of fire. And Hosea exclaims " O death where is thy sting, O grave where is thy victory?" The ravages of death and the grave are repressed at the Reformation, beginning in the sixteenth century. At that time the nations rise from the power of death and the grave, or they enjoy a resurrection.

Power was given to this rider over the fourth part of the earth. This is a fourth part of the old Roman empire as it existed when the prophecy was given. The fourth part was the Western Empire with a

4

part of Spain and Africa given over to the Arabs. But for the loss of Spain and Africa, it would be termed the third part. "Power was given to him to kill with the sword, and with hunger and with death, and with the beasts of the earth."

The term here translated sword is never used in the New Testament, unless in a symbolical sense. The word translated sword under the second seal is not the same as this, and with one exception, in the New Testament, it is always used in a literal sense. The sword of this horseman is the sword of the mouth. Hunger represents the condition of those famishing for the bread of life. Beasts of the earth fitly characterize the cruel governments of the period. The prophets represent such governments as fierce beasts. To kill with the sword and hunger and death and the beasts of the field, means to deprive men, not of natural life, but the life and power of freedom, and of godliness, and of true science.

This rider's career begins about 606 and ends in 1200, and forcibly represents the Roman Catholic oppression.

At the opening of the fifth and sixth seals no horse appears. This may be because no new dynasty is described. It is the same horse or government as the fourth, but there is a change in the condition.

When the fifth seal opens, the souls under the altar speak. Their language shows that it is a period of fierce persecution. By putting into operation the machinery of the inquisition, near the year 1200, the most fearful of all persecutions arose, and it continued for three hundred years. Now hell, or the grave, is satiated.

At the opening of the sixth seal surprising revolutions are manifest. The elevated language suits the subject, and it is such as a divine penman alone can employ. It appears to refer to the overthrow of the debased Roman Catholic and Moslem powers.

The era of great revolutions began in 1500, and the movement continually has increased in intensity. They have the character of a judgment, for the high and the low hide themselves in the dens and in the rocks of the mountains, and say to the mountains and the rocks "Fall on us, and hide us from the face of him that sitteth on the throne, and from the wrath of the Lamb."

XV. THE TRUMPETS.

In Rev. 8, the opening of the seventh seal brings to view the vision of the seven trumpets. Here where the words "a third" is used the application is to a third part of the original empire. It was divided into three portions.

When earth, sea, and rivers, and fountains of waters are mentioned as separate divisions, as is the case especially under the trumpets and vials, they have a specific prophetic import.

Earth means those bordering portions of the empire which are not entirely assimilated in manners and language. Sea means the heart of the empire. It is a center for power, language, manners, and religion. One reason for calling this the sea is the fact that it is near the Great Sea and receives much of its importance from it. Under both the vials and the trumpets there seems to be a literal allusion to the sea.

As rivers and fountains of waters are the same in substance with the sea, the countries represented by them must have a strong resemblance to the center of the empire. They must speak the same language and enjoy the same manners and religion.

Under the trumpets the earth means the Illyrian frontier. The sea is Italy. The rivers and fountains of waters are Gaul, Spain, Britain and Africa.

The earth here embraces some provinces that in the division fell to the Eastern Empire, but this separation was not yet fully consummated.

The Illyrian frontier here styled the earth comprised Rhætia, Noricum, Pannonia, Dalmatia, Dacia, Mæsia, Thrace, Macedonia and Greece. These provinces were the most warlike in the empire. (See Gibbon).

This frontier is properly styled the earth because it formed a great barrier to the incursions of the barbarous nations. By the policy of the emperors, some of these provinces were colonized with barbarians, to prevent the attack of their ruder brethren. This barrier could not, like Gaul, Spain, and Britain, be called rivers and fountains of waters as flowing into the Roman sea, for its center was Constantinople, and not Rome, and its prevailing language Grecian or Barbarian, and not Latin.

The ruin of the earth was due to the Huns. Not that they invaded it first, but they forced the Goths to flee thither for their lives. The ruinous work was begun by the Goths under Fritigern, in the reign of Valens. After the death of Theodosius there followed the direful invasion of Alaric. At length the Huns appeared in person under Attila, "the scourge of God," and they tarried long enough to complete the destruction. The central time of the attack on the earth was 398, or near the date of the death of Theodosius, from which time the fall of the empire is reckoned.

When this angel sounded, "There followed hail and fire mingled with blood, and they were cast upon the earth; and the third part of the trees was burnt up, and all the green grass was burnt up."

In the prophecy of Ezekiel, where he gives a full description of the incursions of the Scythians, he agrees with John, that they come as a cloud and a storm.

The earth was made a desert. The history agrees with the prophecy. It was the boast of Attila that "The grass never grew on the spot where his horse had trod."

In describing the condition of these provinces, after the incursion of the Goths, in the reign of Valens, Gibbon quotes St. Jerome as saying, "Nothing was left except the sky and the earth, and after the destruction of the cities and the extirpation of the human race, the land was overgrown with thick forests, and inextricable brambles."

The saying that "all the green grass was burnt up," implies that the attack on the earth was not confined to the Western Empire. This agrees with th: history. The usual expression "one-third" is not here used.

"And the second angel sounded and, as it were, a great mountain burning with fire was cast into the sea, etc."

A'aric with the Goths, and Genseric with the Vandals, by successful attacks on Italy, and even by pillaging Rome itself, were the chief agents in fulfilling this prophecy. The Vandals subverted the maritime power of Rome. As is often the case, a literal description is here joined with the symbolic.

The movements of the conquerors who directly attacked Italy, were rapid and decisive, answering to the velocity of a mountain hurled into the midst of the sea.

The first movement of Alaric against Italy was about 400.

When the third angel sounded a " burning star fell from heaven upon the third part of the rivers, and upon the fountains of waters."

Here again, is great rapidity of motion answering to the event. This prophecy is fulfilled by the final separation from the Empire of Gaul and Spain, about 407, by the followers of Radagaisus. Near the same date Britain was also lost. Not long after Africa followed.

A third part of the sun moon and stars were smitten when the fourth angel sounded.

This refers to the subversion of the supreme temporal and spiritual authority. Odoacer is the agent.

The fifth trumpet calls forth the Moslem Arabs. They are to torment men five months or 150 years. This begins in 622, and ends a little after the building of the city of Bagdad which was called the " city of peace." During these 150 years nearly all the conquests of the Arabs were made.

It is said that in those days shall men seek death and shall not find it. The Moslem rulers exposed to extreme indignity those Christians that they could not convert to their faith. A desire to die means a desire of the Christians to dissolve their organizations, or to pass out of sight, in order to avoid exposure to continual shame.

Gibbon says: "About two hundred years after Mohammed, the Christians were separated from their fellow-subjects by a turban or girdle of a less honorable color; instead of horses or mules, they were compelled to ride on asses, in the attitude of women. Their public and private buildings were measured by a diminutive standard; in the streets or in the baths it is their duty to give way or bow down before the meanest of the people; and their testimony is rejected if it may tend to the prejudice of a true believer."

As we have already seen, the sixth trumpet is a call for the Turks.

XVI. THE VIALS.

The seventh trumpet introduces us to the vision of the seven vials. This is the third woe. The vials are judgments on modern Rome and the Turk. With particularity they point out many of the events which the sixth seal briefly mentioned.

Like the first trumpet the first vial refers to the earth. We must use the same rules here in locating the earth as under the trumpets. It is the hitherto Roman Catholic countries which are not Latin speaking. These were on the border of the empire of the beast, and were less assimilated, and less servile to the Papacy than the Latin-speaking countries. Prominent among them is England, Scotland, Germany, Holland and Sweden.

The noisome and grievous sore is the peculiar judgments on the Roman Catholics from the period of the reformation. In protestant countries the Roman Catholics were separated and treated like persons having a loathsome and contagious disease. Their institutions were held in great abhorrence. To their great annoyance they were obliged to surrender much of the ecclesiastical accumulations secured by the misrule of centuries.

Like the second trumpet the second vial has reference to the sea. It is those countries which form the centre of the Roman Catholic power, are close to the Great Sea, and are Latin speaking. Among these nations are Spain, France, Italy, Austria and Portugal.

Every living soul dying implies the deprivation of spiritual, moral, intellectual, and political life, which became the heritage of these inhabitants. During the reformation there had been a religious awakening ; before this there had been a revival of letters, but every promise of better things was soon disappointed.

In this prophecy there is also an allusion to the loss of power on the sea, which befell these nations. This began with the ruin of the invincible Armada, and was consummated by Lord Nelson at Trafalgar. This is another instance in which a literal is connected with a symbolical allusion.

Both the third vial and the third trumpet have reference to the rivers and fountains of waters. These became blood under this vial.

It is poured out upon the provinces belonging to the Roman Catholic countries. The symbolical rivers flow into the symbolical sea. These provinces have the same language, manners, and religion as the mother countries. The most important of them are a portion of the Netherlands, and the French, Spanish, and Portuguese colonies in America.

They became blood because of the dreadful wars hazarded to retain them. Also those which were brought under the complete dominion of Rome, assume the putrid and bloody nature of the sea itself. The condition of French Canada, Mexico, and South America demonstrates that these waters are not life giving. The marked contrast, of the unexampled prosperity of the English colonies, of British America, Australia, and especially the United States, is highly suggestive.

The exclamation of the angel of the waters that the Lord has given them blood to drink because they are worthy, refers to the entire Roman Catholic dominion, or to the sea as well as to the rivers and fountains of waters.

The fourth trumpet and vial have a reference to the sun. When this vial was poured out, power was given to this luminary to scorch men with fire. There is blasphemy and a refusal to repent. The sun here is the supreme Roman Catholic authority. Scorching with fire is exercising great tyranny. This scorching is at a time when the people are very sensitive to the oppression, followed by blasphemy and a refusal to repent. The tyranny was of long standing, but the extreme sensitiveness, the blasphemy, and the refusal to repent were most apparent at the epoch of the French revolution. The sun blazed unnaturally previous to his final extinction.

The fifth vial was poured out upon the seat of the beast. The seat of the beast is every place within his dominions where the pope, and kings, and princes rule. This vial is the counterpart of the fourth. In the one the people, in the other the princes are affected. The extreme anguish of the princes, who gnawed their tongues for pain, their neglect of repentance, and their blasphemy, were never so fitly exemplified as during the French revolution. All the rulers, not excepting the pope, were treated with extreme indignity.

The purpose of pouring out the sixth vial was to dry up the waters of the great river Euphrates, and to prepare a way for the kings of the east.

To dry up the Euphrates means to extinguish the

Moslem rule. Kings of the east means the Asiatic kingdoms. To prepare a way for them means to provide for the enlightenment of those who will hear the word, and for the judgment of those who resist it.

The central period for pouring out this vial is probably 1823.

The beast, false prophet, and dragon out of whose mouth proceeds the three unclean spirits like frogs, are the Roman Catholic temporal power, the Papal hierarchy, and the Moslem empire. Unclean spirits like frogs, if they lead men together for battle, do it for no wise or good purpose.

The first gathering at Armageddon was during the. Crusades to drive away the Turk, and the last, equally unwise, and singularly contrasted Armageddon battle was at the Crimea to establish the Turk. In these gatherings there has always been some Josiah in bad company.

The battle of Armageddon was fought in the twelfth and thirteenth, as well as in the nineteenth centuries. As this is the only vial where the Euphrates is directly mentioned, the prophet glances backward to notice a marked contrast.

When the seventh angel poured out his vial there came a great voice out of the temple of the heaven saying "It is done." This declaration delivered in so august a manner was also made in chapter 21. 6 in connection with the idea that the Lord makes all things new.

The seventh seal and trumpet and vial are of the

highest importance.   The seventh seal introduces
the seven trumpets, the seventh trumpet the seven
vials, but the seventh vial proceeds directly to point
out notable and concluding events.

The fact that this vial is poured out into the air
shows that it is more general in its application, and
more active than the others.   Air extends over earth,
sea, rivers and fountains of waters, and the great river
Euphrates.   It is the political, moral, religious, and
intellectual atmosphere that is convulsed.   In the
original, the term translated earthquake is not
restricted to the earth, but it is applied to all things
which can be shaken.

. In Heb. 12: 27, it is stated "And this word, 'yet
once more,' signifieth the removal of those things that
are shaken as of things that are made, that those
things which cannot be shaken may remain."

This vial introduces the greatest earthquake ever
known.   Earthquakes symbolize revolutions.   Then
under this vial we may expect the greatest revolutions.

The meaning of earthquakes is nearly allied to dry-
ing up the Euphrates, the turning the sun into darkness, and the turning the sea and rivers and fountains of waters and the moon into blood.   The
seventh vial describes the central period of the sixth
seal.

The great city here mentioned as divided into
three parts may be the Protestant and Roman Catholic powers, and Russia where the Greek church is
nourished.   Or it may mean the three great depart-

ments of the Protestant dominion, as the British and German empires, and the United States. The rise of the Greek church to such dignity is comparatively recent, or since the expansion of the great Russian empire. In prophecy, city is the symbol of a spiritual and temporal dominion combined.

Then "Great Babylon comes into remembrance before God, to give unto her the cup of the wine of the fierceness of his wrath."

Great Babylon is the Roman Catholic dominion. This came into special remembrance in 1868. The statement that the cities of the nations fell, implies the decay of the Moslem and other powers, which uphold a false religion.

The fact that every island fled away and the mountains were not found, implies the collapse of the mighty and the feeble governments. Mountains are the strong and islands are the feeble governments.

Hail is the symbol for war. Great hail may mean war in which artillery is efficient. The plague of this is exceeding great, and men blaspheme God on account of it. It cannot be said that the blasphemy does not belong to this period.

Voices may mean the intense speech, and writings of men at the period of great awakenings. Lightnings also belong to the period of religious enthusiasm, and may mean the startling nature and the rapid spread of the truth. Thunders follow such a time of moral activity, and may mean the exclamations, and mandates of bodies of excited men, at, or just preceding great revolutions. And often, "*Vox populi vox Dei."* Earthquakes or changes of government always succeed voices, and lightnings, and thunders. Hail or war is commonly another result.

We may be sure that the power of God is manifest in these voices, lightnings, thunders, and earthquakes. They remind one of Sinai and the giving of the law.

Similar expressions are used in other portions of this prophecy. The terms are used just before the sounding of the seven trumpets which began about 400. Again they are used just after the sounding of the seventh trumpet. This trumpet introduces the seven vials. The beginning of the pouring out of these vials was about 1500.

These terms we repeat may have reference to great missionary or revival periods, the attendants of which are voices, or intense speech and writing; then rapid communication of startling truth as lightnings; then authoritative decrees of men as thunder; then earthquakes or changes of government; and then, usually, hail or war.

The first period had its commencement in the days of Christ. The central time of this period for thunders and an earthquake was in the days of Constantine.

The next great epoch takes its name from its chief actor, Luther. The central period for voices, thunder, lightnings, and earthquake was in his day, and the hail followed soon.

The central period for the next epoch is perhaps in

our own day. Now we have the voices, and lightnings, and thunders, and an earthquake and great
hail.

The wonders of the seventh vial are made manifest in abundant useful inventions, the gospel
preached, the Bible circulated, free schools, slaves and
serfs emancipated, the beast and false prophet deprived of power, and the dragon enfeebled. And
other remarkable events may follow soon.

XVII. THE FALL OF JERUSALEM, COMING OF CHRIST, AND END OF THE WORLD.

The Lord said to his disciples, "Ye shall not have
gone over the cities of Israel, till the Son of man
be come." This coming of the Son of man was
probably by his Spirit at the day of Pentecost.

Again when he says to his disciples, "Lo I am
with you alway, even to the end of the world,"
we doubt not but that this presence is fulfilled by
the manifestation of the Spirit.

When the disciples saw Jesus ascend to heaven,
two persons in white appeared, and said, "This same
Jesus. . . . shall so come in like manner as ye
have seen him go into heaven." To some extent
the realization of his presence was enjoyed at the
day of Pentecost. From the nature of the promise,
with their natural eyes, the disciples expected to see
him descend.

Also when he says, "I will not leave you comfort-
less; I will come unto you," he means that he
will come by his Spirit.

In another place when he says, " If I go and prepare a place for you, I will come again, and receive
you unto myself, that where I am there ye may be
also," his coming is at the death of each disciple.

Like the passage in the 11th and 12th of Daniel,
and like the book of Revelation, this prophecy begins with a literal description, but it soon rises to
the use of exalted prophetic figures.

The question of the disciples which the Lord an-
swered is, "When shall Jerusalem be destroyed, and
what shall be the sign of his coming, and of the end of
the world?" For the sake of brevity, in the gospels
of Mark and Luke, these authors have only given
the inquiry respecting the destruction of Jerusalem,
and they have confined themselves to giving only
that portion of the prophecy which was mostly fulfilled before the year 400, or before the destruction
of the Western Roman Empire.

In the prophecy in Matthew, the Lord gives the
sign of his coming at several epochs, and of several
endings of the world. The term used for world is
$\alpha\iota\omega\nu$, and not $\kappa o\sigma\mu os$. He may speak of the ending of the Jewish world, the Roman world, the
Roman Catholic world, the Moslem world, and
finally of the world in the sense of the Christian
dispensation.

He also may speak of his coming with the shout
of war to destroy Jerusalem by the Romans; and
Rome by the Goth's and Vandals; and a portion of
the Eastern Empire by the Arabs; and the Grecian
Empire by the Turks. And he may speak of his

coming with the Archangel's voice, as when Christianity took the place of Paganism in the days of
Constantine. And further he may speak of his
coming with the trumpet of God, as when the
power of Christ prevailed over cruel superstition in
the days of Luther. And certainly he speaks of his
coming when all his enemies are put under his feet.

The assertion that we know not when the Master
of the house will come, at evening, or at midnight,
or at the cock crowing, or in the morning, seems to
imply that he will come at these various seasons.
And hence we should continually watch. The evening may be at the time of the fall of Jerusalem,
and of Rome, and of a portion of the Eastern
Empire; midnight may be at the fall of the Grecian
Empire; the cock crowing may be at the era of the
Great Reformation; and the morning is yet to
come.

In this prophecy scenes are described in the
order of their fulfillment. This may be seen in
every instance, excepting where one description
applies to two or more events.

The Lord cautions the disciples against the de-
ception of those who should come in his name, claim-
ing to be Christ or the Anointed. The caution was
much needed as the events showed at, and before,
the destruction of Jerusalem. The remark is made
that wars, and rumors of wars, and famines, and
earthquakes, and pestilences, should not trouble them,
from the apprehension that the end is near, for they
are merely the beginning of sorrows. The end here

5

spoken of was that of the power of the Jews, as well as that of other persecuting nations afterward mentioned. When great calamities come on men, they instinctively conclude that the end of the world has come. Also the disciples knew of the intimation in Daniel 9 : 26, that the city and the sanctuary should be destroyed by war. They also knew that other oppressive nations should come to a like termination. But they are admonished not to come to the conclusion that every great calamity will be the end of the nation in which they live, or especially the consummation of things.

Then there is a description of persecutions which are to follow. Because iniquity abounds, the love of many shall grow cold. But the cheering assurance is given that he that endures to the end shall be saved. There is a reference here to the persecution under Nero. Those who endured to the end of the Jewish commonwealth were saved; for Vespasian, a humane ruler, assumed the dominion. The same description suits the other notable persecutions. This is the case with the protracted tribulation under Diocletian. Those who endured to the end of Pagan Rome were saved; for Constantine introduced a new order. So at the era of the Reformation. Those who endured the horrors of the inquisition till the end of the Roman Catholic tyranny were saved forever from persecution.

The Lord now declares that the end shall come, when this gospel of the kingdom shall be preached in all the world, for a witness unto all nations.

It is agreeable to the assertion of the sacred writers that the gospel was everywhere preached before the destruction of Jerusalem. So in Col. 1: 23, the apostle says, "Which [gospel] was preached to every creature which is under heaven."

There was another impulse to preach the gospel during the reign of the first Christian emperors, and it was published in all the world before the destruction of the Western Roman Empire, whose capital was Rome.

Again a mighty modern impulse is awakened to preach the gospel in all the world, and before the significant end, this work will be accomplished.

Now there follow a few hints to the Christians which enable them to escape the calamities of the perverse Jews, during the most disastrous siege known in history. According to Luke the "abomination of desolation" was the surrounding of Jerusalem with armies. So the Christians understood it, and at the first encompassing of the city, they fled to the mountains and were all saved.

The Lord declares that "Except those days should be shortened, there should no flesh be saved; but for the elect's sake, those days shall be shortened." The idea is, that if that war, and especially the siege at Jerusalem should be lengthened out, all the inhabitants of the land would perish. But on the account of the Christians who fled to the mountains, and on the account of the remnant of the Jews, some of whose descendants would get converted, those days were shortened.

Luke here introduces the saying of the Lord that "Jerusalem shall be trodden down of the Gentiles till the times of the Gentiles be fulfilled." These times are not yet fulfilled. The completion will probably be at the end of the Moslem power.

A caution is now given against false christs, and false prophets. This caution was needed on many occasions. But the chief reference is made to the distant future as to Mohammed and his followers in the desert, and to the pope and the monks in the secret chambers. These false christs and prophets had power to show great signs and wonders, and there was danger that they should deceive the elect themselves. He declares that the Son of man should not come in such modes. But his coming shall be as the lightning cometh out of the east, and shineth even unto the west. His coming at various times has always been in this mode.

Mention is now made of the eagles and a carcass. This is a proverbial expression. The eagles may refer to the Lord where his power and that of the angels is needed to destroy his enemies, and also it is applicable where his power and that of his angels is needed to sustain his people. When it is said that the Lord comes as a thief in the night, he bears no other resemblance to the thief than that of his unexpected coming. So when he is compared to the eagles the resemblance is only in the faithful watchfulness.

The sun shall now be darkened, and the moon shall not give her light, and the powers of the

heavens shall be shaken. This refers to the obscuring of the temporal and spiritual authority of the
nations in question. In his commentary Lange
says, "Thus when this θλιψις of temptation has
reached its climax, then immediately the great
catastrophe will come." The tribulation of those
days had a primary fulfillment at the culmination
of trial, in the persecution of Nero. Then followed
the destruction of the Jewish commonwealth, or the
obscuring of the sun and moon and the falling of
the stars. After this, is manifested the distress of
the tribes of the earth, when they see the Son of
man coming in the clouds of heaven with power
and great glory. After the Jews were rendered
powerless for evil, the gospel was more successfully
proclaimed.

But this prophecy, by a later event was more defi-
nitely fulfilled. The pressure of tribulation θλιψις
took place in the reign of Diocletian. Then immediately followed the darkening of the sun and moon
and the falling of the stars, or the obscuring of the
Pagan Roman authority, by the es ablishment of
the Christian rule. This was the coming of the Son
of man in the clouds of heaven, with power and
great glory. Then by the messengers or angels of
the Lord from the four winds, there was a great in-
gathering. Great success attended all the efforts to
build up God's kingdom. Now all the tribes of the
earth mourn. The heathen are filled with conster-
nation.

In connection with the assertion that the sign of

the Son of man should appear in heaven, may be mentioned the statement made by Eusebius, that Constantine, and his whole army saw a cross on the clouds with this inscription, *"By this Conquer."*

Tribulation again reached its climax in the horrors of the inquisition. Then follows the obscuring of the Roman Catholic authority, or the darkening of the sun and moon, and the falling of the stars. The reformation succeeds. But this is mentioned further on in this prophecy.

By the parable of the fig-tree, the Lord espe ially refers to the end of that generation, or race, or family of people, as Alford terms it. When all these events already mentioned come to pass, then they should understand that the end of the Roman nation should come. The end of the Roman Empire was sudden and fearful. The overflow of the Goths, Vandals, and Huns was like a flood. He declares that "This generation shall not pass till all these things be fulfilled." He means by "this generation," the world-ruling race or nation, whose capital is at Rome. This race did not pass away till all these things already mentioned, enjoyed a primary fulfillment.

He now declares that no one knows the day and the hour of his coming. As he came when the old world was drowned, and when Sodom was burned up, so in this dispensation, in every judgment of nations, he has come in a time unexpected. But after the event we can explain the prophetic times and seasons.

Yet, though no one knew the day and the hour of his coming, when the event drew near he has given and will give signs by which his servants may know that it is at hand.

As we advance in this prophecy we may observe that when an individual, or individuals, are spoken of, a nation or nations, or a church or churches, as well as persons are pointed out. The prophecy may be applied both to individuals, and to organized bodies, as nations and churches. Unlike some of the prophets he does not use, for prophetic symbols of nations, fierce reptiles and beasts of prey.

The two persons in the field, and the two women grinding at the mill, may refer not only to the separation of righteous persons from the wicked, as in the case of the destruction of Sodom and Jerusalem, but also it may be applicable to two nations or two churches, one of which is exalted to the enjoyment of heavenly privileges, while the other is cast off.

He speaks of a faithful and wise servant, whom his lord when he comes finds providing meat for his household. He is declared to be blessed, for his lord shall make him ruler over all his goods. Nothing more accurately seems to represent the faithful and wise servant, than the Christian Grecian Empire, with its capital at Constantinople. Unlike other portions of the old empire, for a thousand years it was shielded from the plots of strong and fierce enemies.

Now the Lord says, "But and if that evil servant shall say in his heart, my lord delayeth his coming and shall begin to smite his fellow-servants, and to eat and drink with the drunken; the lord of that servant shall come in a day when he looketh not for him, and in an hour that he is not aware of, and shall cut him assunder, [the margin has it cut him off,] and appoint him his portion with the hypocrites: [Luke has it unbelievers:] there shall be weeping and gnashing of teeth."

Here a special reference seems to be made to the Western Roman Empire, destroyed by the northern barbarians, and to that portion of the old empire brought to naught by the Arabs. These two-thirds of the old empire were cut off, and their portion was appointed among the infidels. The weeping and gnashing of teeth fitly describes the anguish of these people. But after a thousand years, his servant, the Grecian Empire, was found unfaithful, and he also was cut off, and his portion was appointed among the unbelievers, or the Moslems.

Now. the kingdom of heaven is said to be like ten virgins which took their lamps, and went forth to meet the bridegroom. A ter the downfall of the Western Empire the northern hordes themselves were converted. The ten virgins are the ten churches existing in the ten nations which made up the Roman Catholic dominion. The bridegroom is Christ, and he came at the era of the Reformation which began with Luther. The midnight is the dark ages. The cry made was that of Wickliffe, and John Huss, and all the reformers of those times. The cry reached throughout the Christian world.

When the Bridegroom came, the wise virgins were the Protestant churches in the five Protestant nations, and the foolish virgins were the churches found in the five Roman Catholic coun'ries. In closing this description the Lord again exhorts to watchfulness, for we know neither the day nor the hour wherein the Son of man cometh. It was Luther's opinion that the Son of man came in his day.

A description is now made of the giving of the talents. As usual, men represent nations. The great truth is made known, that among the modern nations, the most faithful shall be the most powerful. Among these nations, those which most carefully read and practice the divine word, in all things take the lead. This truth should be magnified. Perhaps no more fit example can be found of the person with five talents, and of the other with one talent, than in the case of England and Ireland, and in that of the United States and Mexico.

Now follows the extraordinary description of the coming of the Son of man with all the angels. There is no sufficient authority for terming these angels, or messengers, holy. (See Rev. Ver.) It may be that some of them are not good.. It is the office of evil angels to separate bad men from the good, and to bear them away to everlasting punishment.

Demonology, also sometimes termed sorcery, and witchcraft, and spiritualism, which is a manifestation of the power of demons, or evil spirits, especially since the Reformation, has exerted a most pernicious in-

fluence. Some of these angels may be ministers of
the gospel. In the book of Revelation the pastors of
the seven churches addressed are styled angels; in
another place, in this book, the Lord's ministers are
termed witnesses. These are slain, and after three
days and a half they rise again. This resurrection is
in the age of Luther. For ages till the Reformation
the preachers of the gospel were greatly restrained.
At the Lord's coming in that era they were freed,
and ever since they have enjoyed great power.

Some of these may be guardian angels. In our
times, if, like the servant of Elisha, our eyes were
opened, we should see round about the triumphant
children of the Lord, "the mountain full of horses,
and of chariots of fire." The Lord thus surrounds
his children when he leads them to victory.

When it is said that the Son of man comes with
all the angels, it assures us that there will be a remarkable exaltation of his friends, and downfall of
his foes.

It is said that the bad are cast into everlasting fire,
prepared for the devil and his angels. In one case the
evil spirits, before they are cast out, cried to the Lord,
"Art thou come to torment us before the time?"

It is here declared that the punishment of the
wicked is to be in everlasting fire. The other woes
mentioned in this prophecy are lighter; none of
them are everlasting or by fire.

In this portion of the prophecy there seems to be
a reference to the rewards and punishments that
shall come on "*all nations*" as such. These in-

clude the Protestant, Roman Catholic, Moslem, and Pagan nations. On the one hand there has been shown a due regard to the least of the Lord's brethren, while on the other hand they have been treated with contempt. Some of the nations have been fierce persecutors.

Also there is a manifest reference to the rewards of all *persons* whose love to Christ leads them to honor the least of his brethren, and to the punishment which shall befall all those whose hatred to Christ leads them to despise these little ones.

The punishment here named is similar to that mentioned in the last prophecy, which should come on the beast, and the false prophet, and the devil or the dragon, and death, and hell, and those who worship the beast and his image, and those who are not found written in the book of life. They are all to be cast into the lake of fire. And also " The fearful, and unbelieving, and the abominable, and murderers, and whoremongers, and sorcerers, and idolaters, and all liars shall have their part in the lake which burneth with fire and brimstone." This seems to include all ungodly nations, and churches, and individuals.

It is probable that the coming of the Son of man with all the angels, began at the Great Reformation, and that the revelation of wonders has continued and enhanced till the present. And more signal events are to follow.

XVIII. THE RESURRECTION OF PROPHECY.

It may not be amiss to consider the peculiar import of the resurrection in prophecy.

Doubtless, at death, with a heavenly escort, the good go at once to the presence of the Lord. This was the case with the repenting thief on the cross, and Lazarus, and Stephen. The apostle Paul says: "We know that when he shall appear, we shall be like him for we shall see him as he is." But he appears, and we see him as he is when we die.

No doubt also that the bad, at death, go at once to a place of punishment. When the rich man described by the Lord, died, he "lifted up his eyes in hell being in torment."

There are repeated instances in prophecy of a resurrection which is not a literal raising of men from the dead. This is the case with Ezekiel's vision of the valley of dry bones. As we understand the explanation of it, which the Lord gives, this is not a literal raising of human beings from the dead, but it is the elevation of Israel to the favor of God, and to notable authority.

So the apostle Paul in speaking of the restoration of Israel says :—"For if the casting away of them be the reconciling of the world, what shall the receiving of them be but life from the dead." Life from the dead is a resurrection. Then the restoration of Israel is a resurrection. The sudden conversion, and the remarkable exaltation of the nations is an event similar to the receiving of Israel, and hence it is a resurrection. According to some good expositors, the Reformation, which began with Luther, is referred to in the book of Revelation where the two witnesses, after being slain, and after lying in disgrace three

days and a half, suddenly rise again.   Here is another instance of a symbolical resurrection.

Again there was another resurrection, which was
not literal, which commenced with the prolonged
binding of Satan.   Those who lived and reigned with
Christ a thousand years enjoyed what is called the
first resurrection.

Another instance of the same kind is that of the
beast with seven heads and ten horns.   One of these
heads, which represented Pagan Rome, was wounded
to death, but the deadly wound *was healed.*   Still
another instance is found in Malachi. 4: 5, where
it is promised that Elijah shall come again.   This
was fulfilled by the advent of John the Baptist.

One reason for speaking of the elevation of the
godly nations in obscure times, as by calling it a resurrection, was the jealousy of the rulers.   Any
direct assertion, by the Christians, that they would
soon rule the world would have exposed them to
increased hostility.

The gospel was the power of God to free the soul
from its maladies.   Also, after a few generations,
when the converts multiplied, the tendency of
the gospel was to free them from political bondage.
In the prophetic language they rose from death to
life, or they enjoyed a resurrection.

In 1 Thess. 4: 15, we have the following: "For
this we say unto you by the word of the Lord, that
we which are alive and remain unto the coming of
the Lord, shall not prevent them which are asleep."

"Them which are asleep," refers to those Chris-

tians, who at the time of the Reformation were oppressed by the Moslem tyranny. They are asleep
because they enjoy no civil or religious freedom.
Those who remain to the coming of the Lord, or till
the period of the Great Reformation, shall not go
before these Christians, for under Constantine they
shall have liberty, and political supremacy. This
shall be prolonged in one department of the empire
for more than three hundred years, and in another
for a thousand years. In the book of Revelation
this is styled the first resurrection. In plain language the explanation is this: The raising of the
body politic in the days of Luther, shall not go
before a similar event which must take place in
the days of Constantine.

"Even so them which sleep in Jesus [through
δια Jesus Lange's Commentary] will God bring
with him."

This refers to all those who on account of their
attachment to Christ, either by Pagan or Roman
Catholic persecutors, are deprived of civil and religious liberty. The Lord will bring them with
him, or raise them to the highest authority.

"For the Lord himself shall descend from heaven
with a shout, [shout of war, Conybeare and Howson,]
with the voice of the archangel, and with the trump
of God."

When the Lord comes with a shout of war, he
brings actual war on his enemies to their destruction. One instance was at the downfall of the Jewish commonwealth at the hands of the Romans,

and another was at the ruin of the old Roman
Empire; first by the northern barbarians, secondly,
by the Arabs, and lastly, by the Turks.

The coming of the Lord with the voice of the
archangel was realized in the era of the Christian
freedom which began in the days of the first Christian emperor.   There is a reference to this same
event in the book of Revelation, where the archangel is represented as contending with the dragon.
This is the only place in this book where the archangel is mentioned.

When he descends with the trump of God, the
event seems to be realized in the Great Reformation
under Luther.   This is the last trumpet, and is the
herald of events till the consummation of things.   In
the final prophecy it is termed the seventh trumpet,
and when it sounded great voices in heaven said:
" The kingdoms of the world are become the kingdoms of our Lord and of his Christ, and he shall
reign forever and ever."

" And the dead in Christ shall rise first."

In Rev. 20 : 5, the resurrection which began in
the reign of the first Christian emperor, is called
the first resurrection.

" Then we which are alive and remain, shall be
caught up together with them in the clouds to meet
the Lord in the air; and so shall we ever be with
the Lord."

In Rev. 11 : 12, where the same event is alluded
to, it is said that the two witnesses after being slain,
and after lying three days and a half, came to life

and went up to heaven in a cloud. Clearly there seems to be a reference to the Great Reformation. At this time the nations in Northern Europe began to enjoy political and religious life. The expression, "and so shall we ever be with the Lord," implies that unlike the saints at the first resurrection, who enjoyed political and religious liberty, and exaltation over the nations for only a thousand years, the saints at this resurrection shall enjoy these things forever.

Being caught up in the clouds to meet the Lord in the air, means to be exalted to the enjoyment of the highest authority. This the Protestant nations have long possessed.

In the 15th of 1 Corinthians, the apostle mostly discourses of a literal resurrection till he professed to show a mystery, and then he speaks of a symbolical resurrection.

"We shall not all sleep, but we shall all be changed."

Such authors as Meyer, Winer, and Kling, (see Lange's Commentary), insist on it that the proper translation of the Greek text is, " We shall not all sleep, but we shall be changed." The meaning is, that at the Great Reformation the chosen nations shall not lie dormant, but shall awake to the enjoyment of liberty and power.

"In a moment, in the twinkling of an eye."

The revolution in the days of Luther was sudden.

"At the last trump."

This was the seventh trumpet of the book of Revelation. It was the herald of the Reformation.

The events which belong to this trumpet still continue.

"The dead shall be raised incorruptible, and we shall be changed."

The import of this is, that unlike all the godly nations of former times, those now raised to life or to the possession of freedom and power, shall never lose it. To the same effect Daniel (7 : 18) declares: "But the saints of the Most High shall take the kingdom and possess the kingdom forever, even forever and ever."

"O death where is thy sting! O grave where is thy victory!"

Here this passage refers to natural as well as symbolical death and the grave. But in the original application, (Hosea 13: 14), there was a special reference to the elevation of the nation Ephraim. It was written near the downfall of the ten tribes. In the same chapter it is said: "When Ephraim. . . offended in Baal he died." At the time the prophet wrote he referred not so much to natural life and death, as to the moral, intellectual, and political life and death of Ephraim.

In distinct terms other prophets speak of the restoration of Ephraim after his downfall. The last blessing, both of Jacob and Moses on the twelve tribes, shows that Joseph was to be a special favorite. From thence was to be the shepherd, the stone of Israel. Blessings were to come on him unto the utmost bounds of the everlasting hills. It is also said of him, that with the horns of the unicorns he

6

shall push the people together to the ends of the earth.

Blood will tell. The enterprise of the Israelites has always been irrepressible. It is not improbable, that with a dread of the approaching Scythians, soon after the dispersion, a portion of the ten tribes joined the neighboring Gentile peoples in their immigration to Europe. Nor should it surprise us, that by the blessing of God on these sons of Israel, they should rise to supreme dignity and power.

With no apparent purpose to prove their identity, Dr. Lyman Beecher in his discourses, finds striking resemblances between the Anglo-Saxon Puritans, and the Hebrews.

In Dan. 12:2, it is stated that "Many of them that sleep in the dust of the earth shall awake, some to everlasting life, and some to shame and everlasting contempt."

Also in John 5:28 the Lord says: "Marvel not at this, for the hour is coming in the which all that are in the graves shall hear his voice, and shall come forth; they that have done good unto the resurrection of life; and they that have done evil unto the resurrection of damnation."

Both these passages seem to have the same import. At the death of Christ it is said that the graves were opened. This is a literal fulfillment of these prophecies. He is the "first fruits of them that slept." "Because he lives, we shall live also." His death brought in a new era in which there is specially a glorious resurrection to the good who receive him, and of enhanced condemnation to the bad who reject him. In this dispensation the mode of the resurrection for those who fall asleep as Stephen did, is to see heaven opened ready for their admission, while the ungodly die and forthwith depart to hell as Dives did.

But these prophecies are also fulfilled by a symbolical resurrection. An allusion is made to Ezekiel's vision of the valley of dry bones; to the triumph of the nation Ephraim over death and the grave, as described by Hosea; to the resurrection of organized bodies mentioned by the apostle Paul; and to the first resurrection, the death and elevation of the two witnesses, and the wounding to death of one of the heads of the beast whose deadly wound was healed, spoken of by the prophet at Patmos.

As time advances the glory of the Lord increases. When he was approaching the grave of her brother, the Lord said to Martha, "I am the resurrection and the life." He especially called attention to the resurrection of his children, who at death, instantly rise to glory and immortality. He also showed that he is the resurrection by calling forth Lazarus. Again he showed it at those notable eras when he came with the voice of the archangel, and the trump of God, by raising even nations from the dead. Will he not significantly reveal the same fact at the consummation of his coming, when his enemies are under his feet, and the kingdom is delivered to God the Father.

THE END.

www.ingramcontent.com/pod-product-compliance
Lightning Source LLC
Chambersburg PA
CBHW032358020726
47499CB00008B/2813